I0748618

NO LOITERING

Prohibido Hanguear

Escalona, Esteban (1975)
No Loitering-Prohibido Hanguear [Printed Text]

First edition. New York: Five Points Publishing, 2026. 100 pages; 5 × 8 inches.

NO LOITERING Prohibido Hanguear

250 East 34th Street, New York, NY 10016
USA

Cover design: Camila Jara
Editor: Lenin Brea.
Translator: Aurélie Brambilla.

Back cover texts:
Giovanna Rivero, Bolivian writer. Assistant Professor of Creative Writing and Literature at the University of Iowa.
Pablo García Gámez, Venezuelan writer and playwright. Assistant Professor at Stony Brook University, New York, and at York College, City University of New York.

First edition, February 2026.

ESTEBAN ESCALONA

NO LOITERING

PROHIBIDO HANGUEAR

DEAD RABBITS
colección narrativa

Acknowledgments

To Aurélie Cotugno, for the love she pours into every gesture of her life; for believing in me without hesitation and offering me her unconditional support in the creation of this book.

To my dear friend, Richard Beck, whose attentive eye and insightful words accompanied, with patience and wisdom, the English editing of these stories, guiding them toward their most precise and luminous form.

TABLE OF CONTENTS

No Loitering (Prohibido Hanguear) An Invitation Not To Give Up What You Truly Long For, *by Lenin Brea* 15

There Is Something In Your Basement 19
"ENGLISH, PLEASE!" 35
You're In It Now! 49
Wailing Wall 63
Wine And Spirit 73
The Curious Case Of The Bicycle Cannibals 85

To my mother
who waits for me
at the threshold of home.

To my curious daughter,
for the stories we create together
on every street of a city
that makes us inseparable.

"...And you claim you got something going
something you call unique
But I've seen your self-pity showing
As the tears rolled down your cheeks..."

SIXTO RODRÍGUEZ. Crucify your mind

“No Loitering (Prohibido Hanguear) An invitation not to give up what you truly long for.”

It is a dark fruit I now invoke,
a small circle rescued from the night.
At its summons, we return from wherever we may be
to the very point from which we once departed,
our eyes forgetting where we left a part of ourselves,
to rediscover that unshaken space that belongs to us.

Rolando Cardenas. El fruto invocado

«I had always hoped that this land might become a safe & agreeable Asylum to the virtuous & persecuted part of mankind, to whatever nation they might belong…»

George Washington.

Reading No Loitering (Prohibido Hanguear) means stepping into the shoes of a father fearing to lose his daughter because he is a foreigner; of a real estate agent willing to do whatever it takes to escape the murky circumstances of a large deal in a metropolis she has yet to call her own; of someone who comes to understand that no matter where you are, destiny hinges on an act of faith that brings forth the miracle; of someone who, though unsure of what they're searching for or why, still manages to find love; of someone who, in trying to find their place in the world, ends up losing even their sanity; of someone who resists change in the face of new circumstances and the barrier of language, yet persists in adapting; of someone who experiences the strangeness of a city like New York, with its almost supernatural appetites. In a word, it is about those who confront their immigration reality armed only with the strength of their longings and desires.

No Loitering (Prohibido Hanguear) is not merely an invitation to understand the migrants' situation through the fictionalization of an experience that blends the familiar with the foreign. It is a complicit exhortation to persist, to persevere, to never give up on what is truly longed for. In each of the six stories that make up the book, and from their epigraphs, Escalona makes us feel the vital force born from the clash between what is lost and what is yearned for, between origin and destiny, that power we call desire.

"The migration process is like mourning; it resembles the feeling after the death of a loved one," "sometimes, all it takes is a smile to move forward," and it always comes down to solving the difficult equation between what is left behind and what is desired. This is the common ground for the protagonists of the stories, for whom reality is shaped by the desire that drives them to go beyond.

At the same time, the heroes of the tales in this book are agents of a unique quest, whose journey

— full of contradictions, hesitations, and uncertainties — Escalona masterfully portrays in that liminal space where fantasy — even hallucinated — and reality — even ineffable converge.

Thus, Manhattan and, more broadly, New York are not mere backdrops decorating the protagonists' adventures, but vital and sometimes deadly spaces defined by the encounter, juxtaposition, and divergence of the characters' desiring trajectories; a sort of kaleidoscope of images from the present and the past in perpetual motion and reconfiguration, where the fate of the heroes is at stake: "New York is a fantasy, a metropolis of constant fleeting and abandoned loves seeking conversation in any random bar."

In this, his third book, Escalona gives a refined and original shape to his literary explorations. No Loitering (Prohibido Hanguear) is crafted from various subgenres of fiction and narrative experiments unified by a matured voice. The great metropolis, its margins, and the lives of its inhabitants were the protagonists of Ciudad Capital (2011, 2013, 2023), the author's first book, awarded by the Chilean Ministry of Education. In 2024, he published the bilingual collection of chronicles Tal vez Manhattan / Maybe Manhattan, where he explores Latin American New York through the lens of subjective lived experience, while never losing sight of the intrusion of the fantastic. With No Loitering

(Prohibido Hanguear) we witness a display of his passion "for telling the shadows of great cities and revealing the lives of those who remain invisible in the urban whirlwind."

This work arrives at a difficult moment for migrant communities in the United States, where intolerance and racism have become government practices aimed at denying the rights, dreams, and aspirations of Hispanic communities, but also of a society shaped by multiple migrations. It arrives precisely now, as if by fate, because it was not written for this unfortunate moment, yet it has much to say about it. The reader will realize that this is not a book seeking controversy, but empathy, communication, and dialogue—even beyond the "language barrier."

In this sense, it affirms that the migration issue will not be resolved by denying the other, especially the powerful influence of Spanish on American cultural life. Language is the preferred form of expression of the persistent desire in migrant life, which, tirelessly and against all odds, insists on expressing itself and blending in: "—Should I start the engine?/ —Oh, man, speak English. We are in America!/ —Oh, yes, yes, in America. Sorry, señorita."

Lenin Brea
Editor

THERE IS SOMETHING IN YOUR BASEMENT

It is December in Manhattan. The cold freezes the reddened faces of New Yorkers, the sun dislodges small patches of snow from the rooftops, and on the corner of 39th Street and Lexington Ave, a man gazes at his reflection in the CVS window display, cluttered with gifts and small figurines of saints dressed as surfers, soldiers, or chefs. There is also a Snoopy who, at the push of a button, dances to the rhythm of Jingle Bells. He takes a shaky breath and tries to calm himself after running several blocks, dodging people, puddles, and patches of ice on the sidewalk. He takes another breath. He tries to steady himself with a deep inhale, but it is difficult, the vapor from his mouth rises like a cloud of smoke. The man, whose name is Angel, lifts his gaze to the top of the Chrysler Building, which, up there, stands like a melancholic and lonely hermit among so many gray dwarfs.

Christmas and its joy hurt when you are far from home.

He arrived in the city two years ago and, to his misfortune, just days before the COVID shut down. During the first year, he burned through most of his savings renting small rooms in different Midtown apartments. When the money ran low and he was forced to rent couches for thirty, sometimes even fifty dollars a night, his coworkers would ask, "Why don't you look for a room in Queens? The Bronx? New Jersey? It's just across the river." The questioning, disguised as casual suggestions, hinted at what they saw as an irrational choice one many interpreted as arrogance. But Angel wants to be in Manhattan. Some don't believe him when he says where he lives; after all, most of the people he talks to live in Queens or the Bronx. They eye him from head to toe, searching for some explanation. Our protagonist plays it cool. "Did you say Manhattan?" they ask again, waiting for him to contradict himself and expose the lie. But he knows how to dodge their skepticism. With a deft verbal aikido move, he spins a tale about a city-run lottery for renting rooms in Midtown.

And they believe him.

If Ángel chose to live in New York, it was because of a fleeting hallway conversation with a Norwegian exchange professor. "What's a good place to start over?" he asked casually, just to avoid seeming rude as they walked through the corridors of the economics and business faculty where they both taught. And the name New York hit him with the force of a shove into the void that reckless plunge we all seek at least once. It was thrilling. But then, Ángel remembered Travis Bickle behind the wheel of his taxi, prowling through Manhattan's violent streets, murders, pimps, Broadway prostitutes, gangs, and drugs, endless drugs. "Living in a city where cops kill Latinos and Black people just because they feel like it! That son of a bitch has it in for me."

In life, there are decisions that defy explanation and if an explanation exists, it only reveals itself when one stands alone at the edge of the void. Those who have never felt that fear have never truly lived. Ángel is full of contradictions, and sometimes he thinks about his friends back in Santiago, living comfortably with their families. Their cars, their backyards with barbecue pits for weekend asados, fine wine, beachfront apartments. Ángel has no health insurance, and he is over forty. His body has suffered from the relentless jobs he's had to take in Manhattan jobs he was never accustomed to. His knees are shot, and sometimes, the pain of walking is unbearable.

When he arrived in New York, a torrential rain was falling (why is it that every immigrant remembers arriving on a rainy day?). He passed through immigration, claiming to be a tourist. Once outside the airport, he took the E train, which dropped him off at Grand Central. He stopped in the middle of the dome and gazed up at the ceiling's painted constellations. For a couple of months, he lived in Spanish Harlem with a Russian couple until they kicked him out over a dispute involving some Ukrainian girls. He moved in with one of them, but the romance little more than sex and conversations through an online translator lasted only a few weeks before a man appeared, acting like her husband (though she insisted he wasn't). It was all confusing, absurd like a low-budget sitcom. He had to find another place to live. He moved further uptown to Washington Heights, but the constant blare of bachata, salsa, and the sight of addicts shooting up in the streets drove him mad. So he headed back down to the Upper West Side.

That's where Lady Luck finally stopped the wheel in his favor.

One morning, while taking the elevator down, it got stuck between the second and third floors. Just my luck, he thought. He immediately pressed the emergency button. Once, twice, three times, seven times, until he finally heard a voice.

"Are you alright?"

"Yes, I think... Do you speak Spanish?"

"Of course I speak Spanish."

"I need to get out, I'm on my way to work..."

"Are you Chilean?"

"You too?"

"Hueón, you never see Chileans around here, man. You're lucky, I was just about to leave. Give me your phone number, Hueón."

"For what?"

"Hueón, don't ask questions. Just give it to me."

Ángel gives him the number, and within minutes, he receives a few WhatsApp videos of half-naked dancers shaking their asses to Pump Up the Jam.

They became friends, and the Chilean helped him land a better job with an Indian man who owned Natural Deli near Macy's. The tips were good until they weren't. Even though Ángel recognized the same regular customers, the tips started shrinking. Some time later, that same Chilean friend, whose last name was Vergara, helped him find a basement converted into a garden flat in Kips Bay. It was dark and freezing because the boiler had been out of service for months; they were going to tear down the building soon to make way for a newer one. But it was home the best one he'd had since arriving in New York. Little by little, he furnished it with everything people left out on the sidewalks of the Upper West Side and SoHo, where he roamed on Wednesdays after three, scavenging for furniture. During the pandemic, he found a Smart TV, a few framed sketches of streets in Portugal and France that he hung in the living room, a nearly new couch, and a desk that Vergara helped him haul in his commercial van. On top of that, Vergara —who owned a small building maintenance company— had given him a microwave, an electric burner, a set of pots, and even a metal shelving unit where Ángel had carefully arranged his books and photos from Chile.

But eight months later, the eviction notice came. The building was finally going to be demolished.

"It was bound to happen sooner or later," Vergara told him when Ángel called to break the bad news.

Ever since Ángel had moved into that basement, a rat had kept him company at night. "It's not a rat," Vergara corrected him. "It's a mouse." Then he explained the difference. Some nights, Ángel woke up to the sound of it gnawing on the wood. He would get up, grab a broom, and try to chase it down. One morning, he startled awake and found the mouse staring at him, watching him, studying him, its tiny ears perked up, alert. He thought about throwing a baseball at it. Picked it up. Took aim. But the little creature didn't flinch. Didn't scurry away. Instead, it stood its ground, puffing out its chest, daring him. "Are you sure? Is this really how an adult solves things?" They stared at each other, wary, suspicious. Then they kept staring. Until they both fell asleep.

Ángel's apartment has only two double-hung windows facing north. In winter, sunlight barely makes its way inside. But what truly matters to this story is the small bedroom window overlooking the building's inner courtyard. Beyond that dark patio and the brick walls, past the cracks filled with moss, the scattered flower pots, abandoned furniture, and overflowing trash cans, at the very end of it all, there is a beautiful light coming from an apartment, hidden like a miraculous grotto among the shadows of the skyscrapers. There, on the first floor, lives a girl with a pale, slender, and impossibly flexible body. She moves with such effortless grace and beauty that Ángel has no doubt, is a ballet dancer. She never closes the curtains in her bedroom, and when she steps out of the bathroom with a towel wrapped around her hair, she walks around naked. Ángel enjoys watching her athletic, porcelain-like body. She doesn't know it yet, but he calls her my dancer. His dancer is a little shameless because she doesn't close her curtains when she's with a man either. He watches her delicate legs oscillating in the air, imagining the sounds of her voice.

Fridays are party nights. Around nine, her friends arrive, and they rehearse choreography. Then, after a few drinks, they strip in front of the window, trying on different outfits miniskirts, fur coats. Once they're all dolled up, they leave for some party. At dawn, when Ángel opens his eyes, they're back naked, asleep on the bed. They're slender, their breasts small, pink, almost flat. They, too, look like dancers. So, Ángel has named them the troupe. Some nights, when he walks home from the deli, he stops outside his dancer's building and stares at the nameplate on the first apartment: Ap#1 Vasuchenko, D. He wonders what her name could be. Daisy? Diana? Destiny? More than once, he's thought about ringing the bell. But he never dares to cross that line.

Winter nights are the most beautiful with his dancer. When it snows, and the flakes descend in slow motion, the courtyard transforms into a stage. Ángel is reminded of a film, maybe something by Kurosawa and he sits by the window to wait. Then, suddenly, his mysterious dancer opens her window and steps outside, wearing nothing but a fur coat and boots. She stands in the middle of the courtyard and lets the coat slip off. Ángel swallows hard. She begins to move barefoot in the snow, leaving delicate imprints as she twirls, filling the empty space with shifting shadows that stretch and shrink while the snow slowly melts beneath her. Her liberated body, her secret celebration, it's proof that in every corner of Manhattan, life turns into art. Then she stops, reaches for her phone in the coat's pocket, and takes a few selfies. She sends them to someone.

Ángel glances at his phone and smiles.

Mouse watches everything from a corner of the courtyard. But, bored by the absurd scene, he enters the apartment to nibble on some cheese that Ángel always leaves for him by the door. As he chews, he wonders if the poor man has ever been in love. He has vairous uncertain theories, after all, Mouse isn't much of an expert either, despite being the father of over a hundred offspring, sired with ten or twelve females. Since Ángel met Mouse, he has been thinking a lot about New York's rats, and he no longer sees them as just simple rodents. When he walks to work, he watches how they cross his path and follows them with his eyes. He enjoys observing the push of their hind legs, how their tails drag along the ground, and the elastic, nervous movements of their bodies and heads, until they disappear into some hole they've carved into the pavement. On the subway, Ángel stops at the edge of the platform. Mainly at the 51st Street station, where there are the most rats. They scurry about, searching for food among plastic bottles, soda cans, and potato chip bags. Then, when a train approaches and the rails begin to vibrate, they lift their tiny heads and round ears. Their swollen backs gleam under the train's light. Some don't make much effort to seek shelter, running to another track or diving into a hole. They remain still, and once the cars have passed, they resume their routine activities as if nothing happened. But there's something our protagonist has noticed, Mouse hasn't shown up in the basement for days. He fears the worst. Sometimes he stays awake, waiting for him to return. He's left food on the floor, but nothing. He has even bought colored pencils and drawn a few sketches of Mouse on letter-sized paper, which he then sticks on the wall. He has four so far. Some nights, he wakes up thinking he hears Mouse gnawing at the walls, but it's just the street noises, or maybe other mouses.

But on top of losing Mouse, there's something else.

At the Natural Deli, where Ángel works, he has to do everything: brew coffee, clean tables, scrub the bathroom. On top of that, the owner taught him how to make pastrami sandwiches. Raj always finds a way to pay him less, and it's only gotten worse over the months, as he pockets most of the tips customers leave. He knows very well about our protagonist's immigrant situation and takes advantage of it. When a worker questions him about their pay, Raj just replies in a threatening tone, "Maybe you should ask ICE."

This week, Ángel has been in charge of opening the shop at six in the morning. The usual routine. Turning on the machines, wiping down tables, sweeping the floor, checking the bathroom, and hauling up boxes of milk, bread, coffee, and other supplies from the basement. At noon, he takes a ten-minute break. Ángel steps outside, smoking a joint while watching the Salvation Army guy dance for Christmas donations. But Raj doesn't let him finish. "Fucking Hindu. Fucking city. Fucking customers with their dumb tourist smiles," Ángel mutters under his breath as Raj orders him to go down to the basement and haul up ten more boxes the distributor just delivered. "Fucking Hindu.

Fucking city. Fucking people asking for the check with their dumb tourist smiles," he repeats, furious about the stolen tips, which have now gone too far. Up and down, or maybe down and up. Who knows. When he finishes, Raj asks for a favor, to watch the shop while he goes to the bank to deposit some checks. "I won't take more than ten minutes," he says. Ángel, who only wants to punch him, just smiles and replies, "Sure." He then sits on the boss's throne, from where he can see everything, the register, the cold drinks, and in the back, the Mexican guy named Flores making lunches. A few minutes later, he notices the register is open. He stretches his hands toward it and pulls the drawer. He sees a pile of cash, grabs as much as he can, stuffs it into his pocket, and shuts it. Raj returns, and our protagonist heads to the bathroom to count the money. Almost five hundred dollars. He does some quick math and concludes that it's less than what Raj has stolen from him in tips, but still, it's better than nothing. He steps out of the bathroom, and Raj yells at him from the counter. Ángel snaps out of his trance and remembers the camera behind the register. "Son of a bitch, he saw everything," he thinks. Then, he hears more shouting. Our protagonist, who was never much of a runner, and even less so now with his injured knees, grabs his coat and bolts out, leaving behind the furious screams of the Hindu:

"Fucking thief! Fucking immigrant!" "I'll kill you!"

Ángel ran without stopping, without looking back, as if the devil himself were chasing him. He passed 39th Street, cutting through clouds of steam rising from a manhole, slicing through their fragile shapes. He ran through a few red lights; a taxi driver rolled down his window to yell something, but Ángel didn't hear it. He leaped over puddles of water that reflected his legs on Madison Ave., dodged several cars on Park Ave., and finally reached Lexington Ave., nearly out of breath. He had to steady himself against a CVS window. When he finally mustered the strength to lift his gaze, he saw it: the Chrysler Building, its majestic Art Deco rocket tip and its inquisitive gargoyles watching like judges over the city. "I'm in New York," he whispered. Then he stepped forward for a better view, stretching his back. "Fucked, but in New York!" He laughed in the anonymity of the city, his laughter reflected in the window with its Christmas discounts. He felt better. He breathed more calmly and walked slowly back to his basement, where he felt safe because he had given Raj a different address.

And there, he stayed locked up.

Three or maybe four days passed, spent thinking of ways to return to Chile. He made a list in a notebook and wrote: "Sell furniture, withdraw money from the bank, say goodbye to friends, find cheap flights." His stomach felt so tight that not even a crumb of bread would have fit inside. He sought comfort in his dancer. But she wasn't there, he hadn't seen her in days.

What other sign did he need?

On Sunday, he finally left his trench. It was a sunny but freezing day. The thermometer read 29 degrees Fahrenheit. He woke up starving. Starving. He thought a walk along the East River might do him good, so he took one. Then he went to Trader Joe's and bought some frozen food to heat in the microwave. When he returned to his basement, he got a call from Vergara.

"Did you get the notification?"

"Why are you asking stupid questions?"

"No, man, I mean the latest one... The demolition has been suspended. The owners of the building next door, some Jewish guys, filed a lawsuit and managed to halt everything. I think this is going to drag on. Maybe a couple of years. You've got some serious luck, man."

Ángel didn't let him finish. He hung up the phone and rushed out of his basement, heading for the subway. At the Burlington store in Union Square, he used the stolen cash to buy a shirt, matching pants, a wool coat, and a sweet-scented cologne. Then he went to the shoe store in the same building and bought an elegant pair of brown leather shoes. With all those bags, he returned to his apartment. He showered, shaved, and dressed in his new outfit. But his entire ritual was interrupted by Mouse's sudden appearance. "You're alive!" he shouted with joy. Mouse, feigning indifference, wandered through the tiny apartment, inspecting everything, complaining about the dirty dishes in the sink, the unmade bed, and the wrinkled clothes draped over the sofa. Then he sat by the window overlooking the inner courtyard. Ángel felt happy. And so did Mouse, though he hid his joy by staring out the window. Before leaving, Ángel set out some food, which Mouse acknowledged with a rodent-like smile.

Ángel walked to Park Avenue, bought some flowers, and with them in hand, made his way to his dancer's building. He waited for someone to leave so he could slip inside. He walked down the hallway to the very last door. Unbuttoning his coat, he rang the doorbell, which set off a barking dog. He heard the light, bare footsteps of his beautiful dancer approaching. Ángel shuddered when a voice near the door said, "Hello?" Then the lock gave way with a suspenseful slowness that made him impatient, ending in a glorious click! Once again, the woman's voice, now more playful, "Hello?" She hesitated a few seconds before finally opening the door, looking surprised just before Ángel grabbed her waist and kissed her, leaving no space for his beautiful dancer to even attempt to understand what was happening. She pushed him back and stepped away, so shaken that she let out a breath so powerful it traveled down the hallway, zigzagging, bouncing off the walls until it finally found the exit. And on 33rd Street, it rose into the sky, exploding into hundreds of lights like sparklers scattering through the streets and avenues of Midtown. One of them swooped low over Lexington Ave., passing two strangers who, after exchanging glances, kissed bewildered by the wild spontaneity of their actions. An ambulance driver, captivated by the sight, slammed on the brakes, triggering a traffic jam of epic proportions. The back doors of the ambulance swung open like the curtains of Radio City Hall, and injured musicians, despite their wounds, scrambled to retrieve their instruments and began to play a bolero. The melody was so enchanting that a fruit vendor abandoned his stall and ran after the woman who had never bought anything from him. He called her name, took her hand, and they danced, certain of their desires. She smiled at him in such a beautiful, radiant way that the hurried passersby stopped in their tracks, cheering for the sheer beauty of the moment a rare spectacle in a city like New York. Meanwhile, far from the chaos, the street carnival, Ángel and his beautiful dancer gazed at each other, smiling beneath the doorway. Then, she invited him inside. And only then did Ángel Ernesto Cortez Miranda understand that destiny was nothing more than an act of faith to endure, to believe, and to keep moving forward. But he also knew, without a doubt, that his beautiful dancer was his.

And perhaps, she always had been.

"ENGLISH, PLEASE!"

"I'll go with you on Thursday," is the last thing Deyanira says before leaving. Her voice and the slam of the door shake the shutters and Carlos, who can't think of anything but a warning. But, "Where to?" That question leaves an urgency in his body, distracting him from the news broadcast the images of the young German woman murdered in Brooklyn and the police officer standing next to the body, signaling the cameraman to step away from the crime scene. The anguished voice of the Univision journalist reading out the details of the homicide adds a desolate tone to the crime scene, making the question even more unsettling: "Where does she want to go with me?" Carlos keeps drinking his coffee. He takes sluggish bites of a buttered toast that crumbles between his worker's hands while the news transitions from crime reports to the traffic update. "Where to?" And it's those images of long lines of vehicles on the Long Island Expressway that bring it back to him a sharp pain in his stomach kills his appetite.

"Shit."

Carlos and Deyanira haven't spoken since the last family birthday, and that "I'll go with you on Thursday" is the closest they've had to a conversation.

Deyanira comes home late every day from her job at the marketplace on the corner of 96th and Lexington, where she works as a cashier. On Sundays, they go together to the Spanish mass led by Father Sarmiento and exchange the sign of peace, her looking one way, him the other. They take communion and then kneel, lost in their own tribulations. Carlos closes his eyes and asks God for his problems to disappear once and for all. But he offers nothing in return. Not even a candle to one of the saints. When they get back to the apartment, lunch turns into an ode to indifference. Sitting across from each other at the small table, they avoid eye contact by staring at their phones, making theatrical gestures as they scroll up, then down, then type a message, a fake laugh, then back to scrolling, searching for a new excuse not to talk. After eating, they get up,"Thank you very much." "You're welcome." Carlos heads off for a nap, phone in hand, thinking that María might call at any moment. Sundays are harder because they're both in the small apartment, trying to avoid each other trapped in this tiny battlefield of urban combat. Sometimes, Carlos or Burro, as his friends call him, watches Chelsea, the neighbor's cat, trying to figure out how she sneaks into their apartment and moves through every room unnoticed, leaving only a few hairs on the carpet as proof of her presence. Carlos and Deyanira, on the other hand, are like two eighteen-wheeler trucks, always just millimeters away from a collision.

It's true they haven't spoken since Carlos's brother's birthday. It's also true that since that day, their fights have escalated as Deyanira kept looking for explanations that never came, until her patience finally exploded during Halloween:

"And you? Can't you use your head to learn English?" Deyanira snapped. "It's been ten years, and you still can't understand a simple question, Bu-rri-to."

The argument had started at the neighborhood deli because the cashier didn't speak Spanish and had asked Carlos some questions in heavily accented English. He glared at her and then turned to Deyanira to translate for him. That was enough to push her over the edge. The argument escalated with shouts back and forth until they reached the entrance of their building, where Deyanira criticized his lack of effort in learning English. A few meters away, an Ecuadorian family barbecuing near the parking lot turned around, pretending to grab some beers from the cooler just to get a better view of the fight.

"And how is it my fault that the Chinese lady doesn't speak Spanish? No one speaks English here! In Queens, you don't need to speak English, nobody does!" he retorted, eyeing his neighbors to make sure they knew exactly who was in charge, before yelling at them: "What the hell are you looking at?"

Deyanira grabbed the hem of her skirt and marched toward the building stairs, stopping abruptly.

"But your daughter doesn't speak Spanish. And then you complain, Burro."

"You and your stupid idea of hiding her Spanish. You and your fears. And now my daughter..."

Carlos stopped his rambling when he saw Deyanira's face, how it crumbled into pieces of bitterness that ran down her cheeks to the floor, completely throwing him off. He thought he would receive a harsh response, but that wasn't the case.

"My María..." Deyanira sighed. "Why did you let them do that to her?"

In the weeks following that argument, Carlos was fired from his job, and his daughter, María, left the apartment. That afternoon, Carlos planned to get home early after finishing some electrical installations in a downtown penthouse when Vergara, the owner of the building service, called him to the office. He felt something was off the boss, always ready with a double-entendre joke, no longer sounded playful, and Carlos sensed something bad was coming. "We're broke," Vergara told him bluntly. Carlos didn't know how to react. But then something strange happened, he felt that revitalizing energy that sick people experience before they die, that calm before the storm. "Boss, everything will work out, everything will be fine, you'll see."

For weeks, Carlos moved through Queens, the Bronx, Brooklyn, even New Jersey looking for work. Weeks turned into months, and months into seasons of accumulated anguish and rage. Sometimes he visited his friends in construction to see if there was a handyman job available. He even visited his brother-in-law, a realtor in Astoria, whom he hadn't seen since that birthday party. But the answer was always the same: "There's no work. "Time passed, but his desperation remained. Deyanira was also desperate, even more so after María left for Allentown. "Allentown?" Carlos asked when Deyanira told him, then tried to type the city's name into Google Maps. He had never imagined his daughter would move beyond Long Island.

It was close to Christmas when María called her mother. They talked about the rent in her new apartment while she showed the bedrooms and the kitchen overlooking a park full of trees through the camera. They talked about her new job at the hospital, in pediatrics, and how peaceful everything was so different from Queens, while Carlos listened with the face of a wounded man. No matter how hard he tried, he couldn't understand a single phrase of the conversation. They spoke in Spanglish, and their complicit giggles enraged him. "No, sir, no one mocks me," he stormed into the conversation, only to grow even more frustrated when he couldn't tell his daughter how much he missed her, while she constantly interrupted with, "I don't understand you, Carlos. Speak slower, Carlos." "Carlos? Who do you think you are? I'm your father, you insolent brat," he shouted, but then he couldn't contain the powerful response that came back in English. It couldn't have been anything good, because Deyanira looked up at the sky, asking God for forgiveness, then glared at Burro with a hatred she hadn't felt since that last family birthday.

What happened during that past birthday was something confusing. But confusing only for Carlos' family, because family unity was more important than any personal pain. A survival method that had worked for generations. It was during that late August birthday, while María was preparing the meat for the barbecue, that the confusing event took place. Carlos' family uncles, grandmothers, and cousins—was in the backyard, gathering the last candies from the broken piñata, when Carlos' brother went to talk to María, who was seasoning the meat in the kitchen.

"What are you doing?" he asked, exhaling a strong smell of alcohol.

María looked at him with disdain, the same she had always felt for him, and grabbed the tray of meat to flee.

“Don’t go, we never talk anymore, niece.” His imposing figure, so different from Carlos,’ intimidated the young woman, who stood frozen, gripping the tray as if it were a weapon she could never use. That’s when Deyanira entered the kitchen.

“What are you doing?” the mother shouted, her voice like a commander’s, while he backed away, removing his hands from her daughter’s breasts.

“Nothing, woman, you can’t even have a peaceful chat with your niece anymore,” he replied with a drunken, ironic smile.

Deyanira hugged her daughter while he slowly slipped away, muttering curses under his breath. Then she called Carlos with terrified screams that startled everyone in the backyard still gathering the last piñata candies. Carlos calmed them with a clumsy excuse: “She saw a huge cockroach,” and his relatives laughed at his remark. When he entered the kitchen, they were still embracing, and María was trembling, hiding her face in shame. “It must be a mistake, we’re all family.” “But Carlos” “No, woman, let’s not start with problems again, not now.” He hugged them both and took the meat to the patio, leaving them there, alone, waiting for a response that would never come.

But a few weeks ago, God had finally remembered Carlos’ prayers.

The messenger was Pedro, his neighbor. That day, he called to offer him a job at LaGuardia Airport, parking cars for guests at the IBIS and Aloft hotels. Carlos saw the opportunity to work in something easy, close to home, and with good pay. "The tips are great," Pedro told him. He had worked there years ago and gave Carlos an excellent recommendation to his boss: "Burro is hardworking and honest." They hired him, but there was one problem one he only confessed after the interview: he didn't have a driver's license. That same day, Carlos scheduled an appointment at the Department of Motor Vehicles to take the test, and Deyanira found out everything from the letter that arrived days later, confirming the time and place of the exam: Thursday at 10:30 AM.

"Shit!"

Carlos leaned back in his chair. "Is she going to accompany me to the driving test?" He cursed, mumbled, and mocked himself, thinking it was a date with the devil. "No way out of this, Not even the Virgin can save me now!" Resigned, he left his buttered bread on the plate and turned off the TV just as the Univision news switched from Long Island Expressway to Manhattan traffic. Then he remembered he had to call Pedro to ask for a car to practice with.

Days passed as always tense, distressing, without looking at each other, without speaking, just surviving in a setting they no longer wanted, where the photos of their parents hanging on the walls of another world betrayed past and present realities at once. The day of the test arrived. Carlos and Deyanira left early for the DMV. She, always silent, enjoyed her husband's clumsy behavior. Carlos locked the apartment door, then hesitated. "Wait, I think I forgot to lock it," he told her, running back upstairs to check. Then they took the bus to the airport, where Pedro had secretly taken out a car from the parking lot for them. On the bus, Carlos checked his documents over and over. He spelled them out, making sure they were the right ones, then tucked them into his wallet. A few moments later, uncertainty took over, and he pulled them out again. Deyanira watched him as she popped a mint into her mouth. Carlos shot her a sideways glance, irritated, convinced that she was enjoying the whole thing. At LaGuardia, Pedro was waiting with a Toyota Prius. Carlos had never driven an electric car before, and when he turned it on, he thought the battery was dead. Nothing. No sound. Deyanira, sitting next to him, looked concerned:

"You forgot how to drive now, Burro?"

"It won't start."

Pedro, waiting by the parking lot entrance, looked at them anxiously and gestured with both hands for them to hurry before his boss arrived. Carlos pressed the accelerator, and the car jolted forward, causing Deyanira's head to snap back before it started moving smoothly.

"Look at the dashboard! The dashboard!" Pedro yelled as Carlos drove past him. There, he could check the car's vital signs.

By the time they arrived at the DMV, it was almost ten. The murmurs of the human swarm inside suddenly died down when one of the examiners appeared. She scanned the room, then read from a clipboard and shouted:

"Mr. Carlos Miranda...! Carlos Miranda!" The second time, her tone sounded more irritated.

The woman, a tall, solidly built Black woman, had a purple silk scarf tied around her neck and wore a gray skirt, short enough to reveal a snake tattoo curling around her thigh. She scanned the space like a predator searching for prey, until she found it in the small man hesitantly walking toward her.

"Follow me!" she ordered without even looking at him.

Carlos remembered Pedro's advice be polite at all times. When the woman got into the car and settled into her seat to write some notes, he hurried to advise her:

"Please, put on your seatbelt."

"You won't tell me what I have to do." Carlos didn't fully understand, but her tone made it clear she was annoyed by the suggestion.

"Enciendo el motor?"

"Oh man, speak English. We are in America!"

"Oh, si, yes, in America. Sorry, señorita."

"English, please..."

Carlos tried to think of something to calm himself. He remembered when María used to crawl around the apartment, chasing the little rubber ball he had bought at the fair, laughing with the boundless energy that only toddlers have. The thought made him happy, and the car started moving. He turned onto Jamaica Avenue, following the examiner's clear and precise instructions without trouble. But when they reached Hillside Avenue, she gave one last command.

"Park the car here, please."

"What?"

"Park the car..." Carlos understood too late and drove past the spot. He stopped to reverse.

"What are you doing?! Don't back up!"

"Sorry, sorry." The engine stalled, and Carlos struggled to restart it as the examiner yelled.

"What are you doing?! What are you doing?!"

"Let's go back," she snapped, now clearly fed up. "Go this way, now!"

"Por aqui?"

"English! We live in America!"

Oh my God! He's the worst applicant the woman had that morning. When they return to the Department of Motor Vehicles, Carlos doesn't even have the strength to get up from his seat. He stays there, sitting, staring at a street that has always been hostile to him, while the woman hurriedly scribbles something on the form, mumbling things that Burro is grateful not to understand, and then she throws it onto the seat, slamming the door as a farewell.

"What did you do to the lady, Burro?" Deyanira yells, visibly shaken, as she watches the woman storm toward the building, muttering curses. I knew it! You always mess everything up, you're useless. I'm calling right now to schedule another appointment.

"No, don't" he replies, his voice so fragile that Deyanira understands it's enough. They leave together. In silence. Humiliated, Carlos drives to the nearest station in Jackson Heights, where Deyanira takes the number seven train toward Manhattan, while he continues to LaGuardia to return the car.

Three weeks later, a letter arrives from the Department of Motor Vehicles. Carlos stashes it in the nightstand to keep Deyanira from seeing it. After the evening telenovelas, he finally opens the envelope to check if they've given him another test date or something similar, and is stunned to find a small plastic card with his face on it. His own driver's license. An ID. He doesn't know how to react to the unfamiliar pulses in his chest, as if it might explode when he reads his name aloud: "Carlos Miranda." He doesn't say a word to his wife. He drops onto the couch, facing the television, but he doesn't turn it on. He just stares at the reflection of his own face on the screen.

Winter in New York is over. The snow has vanished. Queens wakes up to a mosaic of faces and accents navigating the unknown. Groups of Latinos, Asians, Africans, Arabs, crossing the uncertain paths of their dreams among faded streets, cluttered with signs and trinkets that hang with their scents and distant mysteries. A Queens that is a piece of New York and the whole world at once.

"Hey, Carlos, how's everything with Deyanira?" Pedro asks, glancing at a girl in a miniskirt hailing a taxi.

"Good, I guess" Carlos takes hurried bites of his bacon, egg, and cheese bagel while staring indifferently down Roosevelt Avenue.

"What do you mean, 'I guess'?" The girl gets into the taxi, and Pedro turns to admire her long legs. "Ever since you two split, you don't want to talk. Well, anyway, good luck. And remember, it's all about attitude, okay? I need the car back by five."

A train passes on its way to Flushing. Both men fall silent, waiting for the metallic clatter to fade, the deafening noise rattling the elevated tracks. But then, Carlos' attention is drawn to a teenage girl inside one of the train cars. Her smile is warm and dreamy, just like his María's. And he smiles with her, in that way that dissolves the agony. "I'm fine... yeah,

I'm fine, don't worry," he murmurs, barely audible, as if hiding behind the sound of the train still dominating the air over Roosevelt Avenue. He leaves eight dollars on the food cart's counter and walks toward the car parked at the corner of Elmhurst, where he programs the GPS to a hospital in Allentown. But before pulling away, his gaze is caught by the vapor trail of a plane departing from LaGuardia. He follows it with his eyes, never letting go, until it fades completely into the skies over New York.

YOU'RE IN IT NOW!

It's four in the afternoon when Margarita receives the text message. The Friday traffic and the heavy January clouds over Manhattan give her that cozy Sunday by the fireplace feeling. But this time, it's different. She turns up the radio and sings along to that song that reminds her of a high school boyfriend: "Cuando calienta el sol, aquí en la playa, siento tu cuerpo vibrar cerca de mí..." Her exaggerated mouth movements, her gesturing hands, everything draws the attention of nearby drivers. "Es tu palpitar, es tu cara, es tu pelo, son tus besos, me estremezco, oh, oh, oh..." A new message comes in. Margarita never answers calls or texts after three on Fridays, but she glances at the screen anyway. It's Elena. She stops at a red light and reads the message. Her intuition was right. She smiles as she restarts the engine. This week, Margarita has closed two deals worth nearly eight million dollars. Now she's after the third. "Those are the best ones." She watches the cars passing by and imagines herself driving home in a sleek metallic Audi. Just this morning, she had closed her last sale a penthouse in Tribeca. It had been a mess. Almost three months of back-and-forth with lawyers, endless interviews with the building's board, a true pack of dark lords, as she had dubbed them. For Elena, they were simply a bunch of damn motherfuckers. Selling apartments in Manhattan can feel like torture compared to Los Angeles, where a solid deal can be wrapped up in just a couple of weeks.

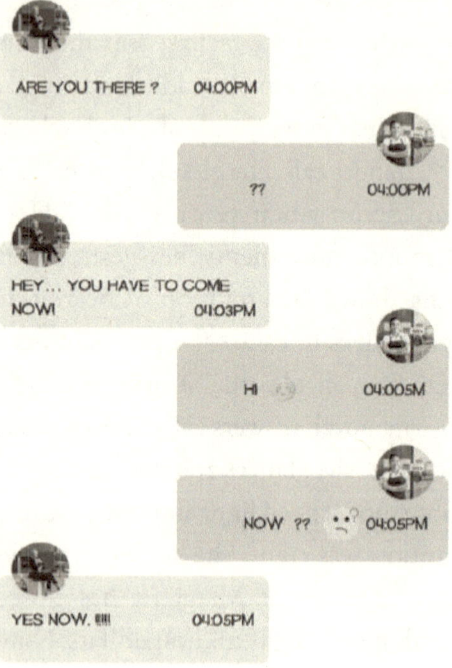

With the phone between her legs, Margarita understands the message. The last time Elena called her with such urgency was to close the sale of an apartment in Hell's Kitchen that had been vacant for two years. Elena knows that she is well known in the industry for her ability to close complex deals, because she has charm, the right words, because she can recognize her clients' weaknesses and guide them toward signing. In no time, the young Texan couple, owners of a digital services company, made up their minds and signed the purchase. This week has truly been legendary. She would surely remember it for the rest of her life.

She knows the address perfectly well, but she still types it into the vehicle's GPS, takes the FDR Drive toward downtown, and sends a voice message: "I'll be there in twenty minutes."

Both of them work in real estate at an office in the Financial District. At very different times, they had each arrived in New York from Los Angeles. They recognized something familiar in each other Margarita's slow, deliberate way of speaking and Elena's distinctive walk. It was during a casual hallway conversation that Elena learned about Margarita's house in L.A. Soon, their conversations expanded to the quirks of New York's public transportation, the warm climate and Mexican food of Los Angeles, the spontaneity of New Yorkers and their obsession with pizza and bagels, the Christmas postcards they had both admired since childhood, and shopping trips to the boutiques in SoHo. And so, three years ago, they began to build something similar to a friendship. Elena doesn't know much about Margarita, things one would typically know in a friendship, but she has learned a lot from her sales techniques, and that, for her, is enough. Margarita knows that Elena is from London, but not really from London, and that she has a Puerto Rican boyfriend who gave her a poodle named Ted. "Like Ted Cruz?" Margarita once joked as they walked to the bar they frequented on Thursdays in the West Village. The look Elena gave her made her realize she had made a mistake.

At 4:50, Margarita arrives at the address. She steps out of the car and takes in the exterior details of the old six story building. It's one of those warehouses built by the Hudson waterfront, the kind that seem to have nine lives. After being abandoned, they were overtaken by drunks, addicts, and gang members who coexisted with the lingering scents of what once filled the space accountants' desks, sacks of coffee beans, Havana tobacco. Years later, those same wanderers were back on the streets, burning newspapers and wooden planks to keep warm. Then came the photographers, writers, and dancers, drawn to the spacious, light-filled lofts, transforming not just their apartments but the entire neighborhood. Trendy restaurants, literary cafés, and alternative designer shops flourished only to be driven out when real estate speculators saw the area as a prime spot for Wall Street executives, making the rents unaffordable. But one nostalgic detail remains, something that always catches Margarita's eye: a large wooden sign hanging from the third floor that reads B-FISCHER & CO. A thin layer of snow covers the sidewalk not enough to make walking in her Manolo heels a problem. She glances at the building's directory, but before she can press the buzzer, Elena swings the door open.

"Follow me, quickly!"

"Hey! What's with all the mystery?"

Elena grabs her by the arm. Margarita averts her gaze from the security camera next to the staircase as they hurry upstairs. On the second floor, they step into an apartment, and Margarita is momentarily mesmerized by its spaciousness and the beauty of its details. But there's no time for admiration. They cross the living room and enter another room with a small library. Margarita glances at the shelves psychology books, English literature, and others with gilded lettering she can't quite decipher. Still wearing her gloves, she pulls a book at random, blows the dust off, and flips through the pages as Elena walks to a desk, where neatly arranged folders and documents await.

"What is all this?"

"I need your help."

"A sale?"

Elena opens a bottle of whiskey sitting beside the bookshelf, pours herself a glass, and offers one to Margarita.

"You know I don't drink while I'm working." Elena shrugs, closes the bottle, and takes a sip.

"It's good. A single malt... but this isn't work."

"Then why the urgency?" Margarita removes her coat and tosses it onto the sofa alongside her purse, a clear sign of displeasure. Elena notices that she keeps her gloves on. She considers asking why but is distracted by Margarita's expectant stare.

"This house belonged to Mrs. McCallister." Elena says, rifling through the documents marked with Post-its until she pulls out a deed. But it could be ours..

"What do you mean? And the owner?"

"She's dead."

"Dead?"

"Of course."

"When?"

"A few days ago. But that's not what matters."

"And what does matter?"

"She had no heirs."

The wind makes strange noises as it slips through the many crevices of the buildings, like a shuddering breath of air. Margarita glances at the books; one by Lovecraft, another by Horacio Quiroga, before shifting her gaze to the exquisite details of the apartment: the decorated cornices, the crown moldings, the plaster columns adorned with fleur-de-lis at the corners, a marble fireplace, and the transparent plastic door handles. The scents of the place intensify, and she hears sounds on the walls, on the ceiling noises that seem to come from everywhere.

"It's just the wind, don't be scared. They say the worst storm in years is coming. Margarita, the tempest has begun." Elena draws out the last words, as if they were a veiled warning, then reaches for the whiskey bottle, pouring two glasses. This time, Margarita accepts.

"How did she die?"

"What kind of question is that?"

"It's just a question."

"I don't know. Her body is in the other room."

Margarita perches on the edge of the couch, glancing sideways at the door through which she entered just minutes ago. Outside, the wind swings the sign of the pizzeria on the corner, the metallic rings creaking eerily.

"Oh, that face, don't be silly. We cremated her. She's in the columbarium, right there in the living room."

"What do you mean, we cremated her?"

"It was last week. I signed the authorization myself."

All those spy and gangster movies Margarita has watched tell her it's best not to ask any more questions. She looks around, and suddenly everything feels... different. The furniture seems to have shifted. The leather couch that was by the entrance now sits near the window. The small bookshelf once beside the fireplace is now near the door. And where there was once a plain white wall, there is now a painting. But the exit it's nowhere to be found.

"It's a nice apartment." Margarita says, slipping into her real estate agent persona.

"Yes, it is. Three and a half million. But I need money for lawyers, for the paperwork. It has to be quick. You know people who can make things happen for the right price. I need your help. A million is yours." Margarita walks to the table covered in folders, pretending to examine them.

"I'm not helping you… but don't worry, I won't say anything."

"Don't be stupid. I know all about your mortgage."

"That's none of your business."

"What are you doing? You can't leave." Elena grabs her arm.

"Why not?"

"Because you're in it now."

The storm begins to lash against the city with an almost supernatural force. Margarita's and Elena's phones buzz with emergency alerts: Do not go outside. But then… a third phone rings. Margarita notices. She reaches for her coat and bag, ready to leave. She looks out the window, her car is disappearing under the snow. Elena watches her with something close to contempt.

"Last week, you signed the sale documents for Tribeca. Remember?" Elena pauses, waiting for recognition to sink in, "I slipped in a few papers for this apartment. Margarita, you signed for all of this. You and I are listed as the buyers of this little gem. So… have a drink. Let's celebrate."

Margarita remembers those documents. And yes, it's true. Damn it. The realization hits hard, but she doesn't bother hiding her frustration. She walks to the bookshelf, making a few deliberate movements, ones Elena has seen before, ones she recognizes instantly.

"There are cameras, aren't there?"

"They haven't worked in ages."

"Okay. Now tell me, how did the old lady die?"

"A heart attack."

"A heart attack..." Margarita repeats, flipping through the Lovecraft book. "I don't know what you're up to, but don't count on me. I have a good lawyer." She shifts her gaze to the desk piled high with papers. "I see you've been planning this for a while."

A noise echoes from the second floor. Something falling, a bag, maybe a suitcase. Margarita looks up.

"What was that?"

"Don't worry. It's Andrei, my boyfriend."

"Your boyfriend?"

"Yes, my boyfriend?"

"And Jason? the Puerto Rican guy from Wall Street?"

"He didn't want to get married, so I left him. Now I'm with Andrei. He's not as smart, but he loves me. He's just taking inventory of the valuables." Elena pulls the curtains closed, but Margarita catches a final glimpse of her car completely buried under the snow. Or maybe it's not even hers.

"You're in it now. And there's no way out."

"I'm in it." Now she feels annoyed, recalling all the documents Elena used to hand her almost at the end of the workday documents she had signed without reviewing.

"The columbarium."

"What did you say?"

"Okay. I'm in it. The columbarium... I want to see it. If we're going to be partners, I need as much information as possible. The more I know, the better. And tell me about Mrs. McCallister. How did you meet her?"

"It's the best decision" Elena said, taking the last sip from her glass before heading to the living room.

As they made their way to the columbarium, Elena told her about her first jobs working as a receptionist at a hotel in Santa Monica, then as a waitress at a French restaurant in Beverly Hills. She recounted in great detail her dreams of becoming an actress, and that's when Margarita knew she had fallen into the trap. After a brief silence, Elena continued, explaining that four years later, she had returned to Santa Monica to work as a nurse's assistant at a senior care home. It was there that she had met Mrs. McCallister.

"If she was from Los Angeles, what was she doing here?"

"When I found out she owned this gem, I convinced her to come. I told her she would live out her final years much better here, and I wasn't wrong she loved it. You know how life is here."

At that moment, Andrei came down the stairs, carrying a heavy duffel bag. Margarita checked her watch; it was 5:40. His muscular body looked clumsy as he descended the spiral staircase with a few objects from the loot, his veins bulging in his neck. The whole scene struck her as absurd, made even more unpleasant by Andrei's greeting.

"Hey, gorgeous!" Margarita smiled but didn't respond. Instead, she looked away.

Elena shot at Andrei a glare of contempt, or maybe jealousy. She stared at him so intensely that he dropped the bag. Elena rushed to pick it up, scolding him in another language. This was the moment Margarita had been waiting for because Andrei looked at her in that way. The signal. She grabbed her purse and slipped out of the room. Elena screamed, furious at Andrei. In the hallway, as Margarita searched her purse for her car keys, she realized she had left them in her coat. There was no time to go back. She rushed down the stairs, letting her hair shield her face. But when she reached the street, she knew she had come out the wrong way everything looked different. She kicked off her high heels and tried to run, but it was useless in the snow. She resorted to long strides down Franklin St., glancing around, trying to get her bearings, but the wind was a barrage of tiny shards stabbing at her eyes and face. A traffic light glowed red in the distance. This could be the corner of Varick… or maybe not. When she reached it, she searched desperately for a taxi. Everything was white. No streets, no sidewalks, just snow. Somewhere, muffled by the wind, she heard a plow truck scraping its blade against the pavement. But she had no idea where she was. The swirling gusts distorted everything. Despite her gloves, the cold was beginning to freeze her hands. Her feet, now soaked, ached terribly. It was a white nightmare, accompanied by a wind that tangled her hair and yanked at her clothes. It felt as if she had landed on an abandoned planet. This is what downtown is like in winter. She thought about screaming and did but it was pointless. The wind swallowed her voice, sealing her inside its cursed void. Margarita ran down streets, or maybe sidewalks perhaps even passing the same spot twice. It was impossible to tell. Then, suddenly, she stopped. A voice. A voice that soothed her. It was 6:20. Andrei wrapped her in his coat. Margarita's gaze turned feline.

"That was fast, wasn't it?"

"Yes."

"Good. Bad boy, I assume you left her in the basement. Right?"

"..."

"See? It was easier than you thought. Well done, bad boy. Well done."

"..."

Margarita hugged and kissed him. Andrei slid warm snow boots onto her frozen feet, and together, they walked arm in arm down Varick, absolutely certain that by the time the pale morning sun reappeared over the restless island, only one of them would wake up to close the sale of the McCallister apartment.

WAILING WALL

After several weeks, her voice seems familiar, and that confuses him as much as the long confinement he has had to endure...

I hear the children running back and forth, their laughter and footsteps filling the space between the walls. Then the woman's voice rises above the commotion, imposing order time to eat, time for homework, time to sleep. Every so often the man arrives late at night, too drunk to stand straight, shouting about something that displeases him, perhaps the state of the house, perhaps the food is not to his liking. He hits her with the weariness of a man suffocated by work, by dull sex, by the monotony of his own existence. I need to listen. I sit against the wall, pressing my ear to the cool surface, trying to catch every sound. These are results of the pandemic the confinement is changing us. My neighbor bought a treadmill, which I hear every morning, and her husband got a massive sixty-inch television to drown himself in action movies. I have tried different positions. Sometimes lying down, sometimes sitting with my back pressed against the wall, and other times kneeling, listening intently through the stethoscope I stole from Nurse Rose. Little by little, I feel my heartbeat slowing, my breath finding the rhythm I need, coming in waves as I inhale and exhale, just as the doctor instructs me during check-ups.

"Inhale, exhale, Elías. Inhale, exhale."

The first time I heard them was on a Friday after dinner. I woke up startled by shouting. I pressed myself against the wall and stayed there for a few minutes, straining to listen but there was nothing. Not a sound. Not even crying. Was it a nightmare? The following night, the voices returned, and I sat by the wall to listen. At first there were only murmurs faint conversations, and hushed pleas that vanished as quickly as they came. Then came stifled sobs and the shuffling of bare feet pacing back and forth.

Sometimes I have nightmares. I hear the rustling of suitcases, hurried conversations, the abrupt slam of a door. Then, a car arrives and leaves in a rush. I remain, stethoscope in hand, listening to the silence of the home, a silence so deep it feels like another world. A loneliness that aches. Other times, I scream at them not to go. I pound my fists against the wall, desperate for them to hear me, pounding so hard that my knuckles split open, staining my clothes with blood, pooling into a dark red puddle on the floor. And then, the dawn comes to rescue me.

According to Freud, in his book The Interpretation of Dreams, individuals suffer from hidden emotions bur-

ied in the unconscious, which emerge encoded into consciousness during dreams. Freud believed that every dream is an interpretable message and that it will have meaning once it is understood.

There are days when I don't feel well and I'm in a bad mood. Everything changed when the man arrived that night. Around eight o'clock I heard his enraged animal-like howling and the woman whimpering. It all happened so fast. I put on the stethoscope, but I couldn't understand anything amidst the woman was screaming and children were crying. Then a door slammed followed by a silence that made me anxious. That night, I couldn't sleep because my headache came back the one that started after what happened at the border over in Sunland Park. Every morning, Nurse Rose comes to check on me. What idiots! They think that damn virus is going to do something to me, Elías Sanchez. But explanations are useless. I have to stay locked up for a long time who knows until when. They only let me out in the yard to get some sun for a couple of hours a day. Vitamin D, they say, is important for health. It was during one of those visits, as Nurse Rose finished examining me, that I noticed the stethoscope hanging from her purse. It was easy because it was right there in plain sight. I just had to stretch my hand out and steal it. There are women who like to be stolen from and touched.

Luckily for me, she seems to enjoy both.

The first effects of confinement began a few days after I arrived. The first week, I confused Thursday with Friday and Sunday with Monday. I had a meeting with my lawyer on Monday, but I waited for him on Sunday without realizing what day it was. So I started making vertical marks on the wall and I crossed every seventh one with a horizontal line.

"And is it working?" Jerry asks me, the cop who comes by every week to check if I'm following my quarantine.

"Of course, you idiot!" I reply with a neighborly smile that leaves him confused.

The only good thing about Jerry is that he always shares his cigarettes with me.

My life in the desert helped me a lot during this confinement. One of the best things I learned at the border was self-control keeping a cool head when needed. I also learned how to defend myself with a tactical knife and how to handle a nine-millimeter pistol. Before leaving that job, I even got to fire a cuerno de chivo, and Jerry knows it. That's why he looks at me with respect. He knows I've got some serious balls. In total, I spent ten years moving packages (our bosses told us they were clients) from Mexico to the United States through different routes. I started as a truck driver and ended up at the Sunland Park crossing. That life wears you down. The violence, the deaths, the fear… I was already exhausted when the business with the boy happened. A ten year old boy, traveling with his mother —both Salvadoran— climbed the wall just the way we taught him. He did it well. But when he reached the top, he stopped to watch the sunrise over the desert. Or maybe he was admiring the way the sand and the wall changed colors. I remember seeing his smile, his face turning red under the first rays of sunlight. That's when his mother yelled at him to move, and the boy lost his balance. He fell head first.

Death was instant.

His mother threw herself over him, gently slapping his face, trying to wake him up. I remember that lifeless gaze that looked as if it had just discovered something strange and beautiful. We all panicked and ran when we saw in the distance the trail of dust from a border patrol vehicle. I don't know if it was out of duty to help a client or pure sympathy, but I turned to look at that mother still clinging to her son on the ground. I went back for her, and through force hitting, shouting, almost dragging her across the desert, risking my own life. I got her to safety. I never went back to Mexico. And I stayed with that woman.

In 2007, Philip Zimbardo published The Lucifer Effect, a book that explains how external influence can trigger a transformation process in which a normal individu-

al can end up committing acts of barbarity, depending on the environment and circumstances they are placed in. In 2005, Zimbardo appeared as an expert witness to defend the Marines involved in the Abu Ghraib prison scandal, where they committed horrific acts of torture against civilians.

Every day I wake up at five in the morning. I do sit-ups, push ups, some boxing, and then head for breakfast. Around seven, I hear the first movements in the apartment. The sound of a pan or maybe a pot, all the same, the woman is in the kitchen. I recognize the smell of breakfast. Her name is María (I know because her children don't call her Mom, they call her María), and she calls out to them: "Adam! Jayden!" I rush to grab the stethoscope I keep hidden under the bed and listen. If it weren't for the fact that there's nothing else to do in this place, I wouldn't even care. Why the hell should I care about people? After all, I'm not a damn snoop. But that night, when the man came home drunk, and I heard his wounded-macho shouting, the scraping of furniture, glass shattering against the wall, and damn! the way he yelled "Whore!" at her, I felt a connection to that violence. That night, I dreamed of them. They looked like a happy family on a summer picnic, with a car, a dog, and a barbecue. I don't remember anything else, just that I woke up sweating and deeply sad. A friend of my wife, the one who lived downstairs, once told me: "You need to try to remember your dreams. They carry messages."

"What the fuck is that?" I yelled in her face, making her back away, frightened. She never dared to come back to our apartment.

"Why do you always have to be an ass?" My wife lamented that time.

"Because I'm like a baby! That's all. Anything else? Okay."

I don't know why she left me. One day, she just didn't come back, and with this whole quarantine thing, they have me locked up here, unable to go out and look for her. But I swear, once this is over, I'll find her. I don't care who she's cheating on me with that damn whore it could be the goddamn president, but she'll pay for it.

One afternoon, I heard María on the phone. Her voice was tense, rushed. From the way she spoke, it seemed like she was talking to a social worker or maybe someone from the police. I don't know about these things. "Yes, the number, I already wrote it down. What time? Yes, three o'clock. Can you repeat the last name? Oh, yes, don't worry, I'm still working on the complaint." Then the door opens, heavy footsteps shake the wooden floor, and the man yells at the woman, calling her a whore (can't he think of anything else to say?). The sharp sound of a slap, the phone crashing to the floor, and then the crying. Thirty minutes later, the police arrive. It's Jerry, with his partner Billy, an overweight, bearded guy who looks like he works at a 99-cent pizza shop. As his big statement, he has a spiderweb tattoo on his neck. They go upstairs to the apartment, and I peek out the door just to mess with them.

"Hey, Jerry! Why didn't you have the balls to be a Marine? Whose dick did you have to suck to avoid ending up as a traffic cop?"

"It's always the same, Elías! Do you think your bullshit provokes me?"

"I don't want to provoke you; I just want to remind you of what you are and why I have balls and you don't" I said while grabbing my crotch.

I heard a voice behind me it was the fat pizza guy. He twisted my arm behind my back, and in seconds, I was handcuffed. And all for sticking my nose where it didn't belong. That bastard Jerry always abuses the drunks, the Blacks, and the Latinos in Hicksville.

"Hey, Jerry, why don't you let go of me and we'll see how much of a man you really are?"

I didn't get to say anything else before I took a hit to the head. When I woke up, I was in solitary confinement, where I stayed for a few days. After that, I didn't hear any more noises, and that's when the anxiety began.

Many people have left the neighborhood, afraid of catching the virus. Many have died, mostly Latinos. I stopped doing jumping jacks, push ups, side trunk bends, and punches. I barely touched my breakfast, lunch, or dinner because I preferred to stay glued to the wall, waiting for their return. But nothing. It seemed they had moved to another county. I was left kneeling, the stethoscope hanging from my hand, drowning in a terrifying sense of abandonment. That week, I didn't go out to the yard either. I just stared out the window at my neighbors, watching them walk back and forth, smoking, talking, or just cursing.

But today, the family has returned.

The children's voices rush to their rooms, the woman's hurried footsteps stop in the kitchen. She sets the bags on the floor. Silence. Then the sound of pots and plates being moved around, the sharp chopping of a knife, then the sink running. I feel happy, a kind of renewed energy, an electric surge. I leap toward the wall, eager to savor every word of their conversations. They had only gone to a friend of María's in Philadelphia. They had a barbecue on Sunday, took the kids to the playground in the afternoons, and did some shopping. María sounds very happy. She talks to her children about the possibility of seeing their grandparents again, about the paperwork to get legal status. But around eight, after dinner, when only the sounds of the TV remain, the man arrives. Everything turns into a mess. Insults, threats, blows. She screams, "Stop!" But the bastard keeps going. "What is this?" He shoves her against the wall. "What the hell is this?" I hear him furiously tearing a paper into shreds, then more blows. Then, it sounds like a sack of potatoes hitting the floor. Shit. My head hurts. "Why the police!? Why? You're going to regret it, you fucking bitch!" That's enough. I have to go beat the crap out of that coward before Jerry gets here and takes him from me. I'll beat him to a pulp, let's see how much of a man he is with me. I try to open the door. It's locked. What the fuck is this!? I throw my body against it, kick it, try to break it down. The woman screams for me not to kill her. Not to kill her?

The woman's voice confuses him. Elías stumbles back at her pleas, her voice like a freshly slaughtered lamb, but he bumps into his cot, looks around, and suddenly, the kitchen furniture blends into the dark, foul-smelling cell.

"What's going on, María? Where am I?"

He looks at the filthy urinal, the graffiti covered walls, the poster of a naked woman, and the other inmates yelling at him to shut up. And María, lying on the floor, beaten and bleeding. Elías feels his legs giving out, trembling, and he drops to his knees beside her. He asks again. And only then does she lift her gaze:

"Do you really not know?"

Wine and spirit

Causalities

It all began at Small, that jazz club in the West Village where I arrived in search of some fun, a party, and, if lucky, the bed of an unknown woman. The city is full of immigrants, and at some point, we are all looking for the same thing. That dark, cramped basement, seemingly built at the very core of the planet, felt like the perfect place. That night, the Blue Notes were playing, and the place was so packed that bodies brushed against each other in syncopated rhythm, so electrified by the music that when it stopped playing, I had to grab onto something to keep from falling. I had lost something important, something deep inside me. I wanted to cry, but I couldn't. I watched the pianist, who was organizing his sheet music, an angel silhouetted against the light; the bassist, fine-tuning the strings of his instrument; and the vocalist, sipping from a glass of water with a slice of lemon. It was time for the crowd to shift, and that was when I saw her. Given the atmosphere of chaos, I swear before whatever god you choose that miracles do exist. A drumroll silenced the murmurs. The bass began to play, followed by the cymbals, and then my body moved with subtle inertia toward that woman. Seated at the bar, legs crossed, gazing absentmindedly at the stage, she looked as if she were posing for a Vogue photographer. In her right hand, she held a short glass, while the fingers of her other hand tapped against the bar, following the rhythm of the music. Oh, magnificent god of the city, who placed that carnival of a woman before me on that night of music and alcohol! Oh, wondrous god, who made me feel like a hunter stalking his prey in the middle of a blues riff! I stopped beside her. She was drinking a single malt. I knew it by the color of the whiskey and the sensual way she resisted its burn as savored it. Her moistened lips seemed like delicate glass, begging to be shattered by my kisses. I closed my eyes, imagining the exquisite taste of her mouth, and reached out in the wicked darkness to confirm whether it was all real.

And it was.

Wine, she said her name was. I thought I had misheard and had to ask again. Wine, she repeated with a smile. Then we listened to the band, talked, drank, and as we left the club, I felt that finally, things in New York might be different.

In my favor.

*

I like to remember the day I met Spirit. I had been kicked out of the room I was renting on Roosevelt and had nowhere to stay. I considered finding a shelter in Manhattan but decided to take a moment to think things through, so I stepped into a café at Penn Station. I had my small carry-on suitcase with a change of clothes and my books, which made it ridiculously heavy whenever I had to climb stairs. On the table sat my little Bialetti machine, wrapped in a plastic bag to keep it from getting wet in the relentless downpour that afternoon. I felt fragile in a city that still seemed foreign, and a sharp edged fear clung to me so closely that I even considered buying a ticket back to Chile. I had enough reasons: my visa renewal had been denied, and I was homeless. It wasn't hard to add one plus one and arrive at the most obvious conclusion. That Saturday, the rain in New York was relentless, and the streets, the buildings, the people, they all had a hostile air. Or maybe it was just the natural attitude of a city so full of desolation. That was when Spirit walked in, dragging a twenty-three-kilo suitcase. She was completely soaked, as if an entire barrel of water had been dumped over her. She left her umbrella by the entrance and went straight to the pastry display. I liked her jet-black hair, cascading down to her slender, distinguished neck. Surely, she descended from some long-extinct South American royalty. When she stopped at the register, I noticed a small tattoo on the nape of her neck. They were meaningless lines, and I played for a while, imagining what they might signify as I sipped my latte. After paying, she turned, tray in one hand, suitcase in the other, scanning the cramped space we were all trapped in. She sat by the window and pulled out a book, flipping through its pages while staring out at the street. Then she put on red-framed glasses and focused on the text with little apparent interest. I got up and went to the bathroom. When I returned, I passed by her table. She was still looking out the window. The book on the table was by Camus, its title in Portuguese. "Sometimes we create exaggerated ideas about what we think we know," I said in Spanish. She turned to me with sadness in her eyes, then smiled softly. I sat beside her, and we talked as if we had known each other forever. We entertained ourselves watching the people walking through the rain that afternoon, inventing stories about each of them based on their faces, their clothes, the way they moved.

Sometimes, all it takes to keep going is a smile.

Faith

After a week of searching for a place to live, I found a small room in the East Village, on Second Avenue and Nineteenth Street. The place is tiny, dark, with a view of a brick wall in the inner courtyard that always seems damp. But it's a good place.

My roommate is a Japanese guy who leaves early every day and doesn't come back until after midnight. I've never seen him, which makes me wonder if he even exists. We made the deal online through a rental page. My room has a small desk, and the day I arrived, I found a box in the closet filled with letter-sized paper and books by Carson McCullers and Joseph Conrad. They probably belonged to the previous tenant. Why didn't they take them?

The moment I stepped into the apartment, I felt like it was made for me. But in reality, any place was better than a shelter or the tiny room I had rented in Queens.

*

Spirit likes my apartment. "It's nice," she says every time she walks in, looking around in amazement as if it were the first time. Some weekends, we rent a car to escape Manhattan. We choose strange and dangerous places, where if a cop asks about someone, the answer will always be, "I don't know anything, never seen or heard a thing." Driving down the expressway on Saturdays, as if fleeing from Judgment Day, we head toward those abandoned apartments, ideal hiding spots for mobsters who need to get rid of bodies. With Spirit, we seek new experiences, let's say, unconventional ones. To get inside, we climb the fire escapes, and I can't help but steal glances up her short skirt, watching with satisfaction as her underwear contrasts against the city sky. She has an uncanny ability to climb stairs, one that doesn't quite match her reserved, academic face. Then we force a window open —sometimes we have to break a pane— and slip into a small room, furnished only with a bed, an old battery-powered radio, and a chair. "O que mais é preciso para amar?" she whispers, turning on the radio to play something by Tribalistas. And we dance, pressed so close together, moving so slowly, so in sync, that soon we are naked, touching, tracing the dampness of our bodies, whispering in each other's ears as my chest presses firmly against her back, as my tense muscles search for a path between her legs, as my hands roam over her full breasts and the reflection of her legendary gaze flickers against the window, against a city that fades away with us. Then Spirit lets herself be guided to the makeshift bed, teasing me with kisses interrupted by slow, lingering bites that drive me mad, even more so when she whispers in my ear, "Não se desespere." Don't be impatient. But that only makes me more desperate, and I grab her hips, pulling her toward me. She gives me a moan soft, almost supernatural, that unsettles the prostitutes outside, sending them running through the streets, searching for a man to love them with that same kind of urgency. Spirit looks at me, bewildered, as if discovering the chaos of her own body. And then, in that final moment, when the city's oxygen is no longer enough, when her hips move with more force, when she lifts her head to the ceiling, when the dim glow of a neon Pepsi sign from the rooftop barely lights the room, in that moment of breathless impatience, she cries out: "My Kairos!"

Silence.

The wail of an ambulance.

The Pepsi sign goes dark.

After a few minutes, we breathe again like human beings. We slip back out the window and sit on the fire escape, sipping white wine and smoking a cigarette as we watch the lovers in the other buildings. She laughs contentedly, flipping through her copy of Clarice Lispector, speaking about the fragility of life. I don't think I mentioned it before, but Spirit is a theater arts professor.

"Is there anything more useless than writing?" she asks me, with a tinge of sadness. I know there's nothing to say...

"Traffic cops?" She smiles and pulls me into an embrace, and in that moment, I feel the city is so beautiful, so unique, that I silently thank the universe for letting me know her.

That night, I notice a scar on the right side of her hip. When I ask about it, she hesitates before answering. "All women carry marks left by men," she says. "Some are hard to erase. Others, like this one, are impossible." She stares out the window, toward the starless sky. I feel ashamed. I feel like a complete fool.

*

Wine and I had an unspoken agreement: every Friday, we'd meet at the jazz club, and afterward, we'd go to her apartment in Tribeca. But our constant desperation to love each other always made us start right there, in the darkness of the club. We touched as if nothing else in the world existed, only us and our desires, trapped in a city full of desires. When we'd had enough of the game, we'd leave for her place. On the way, I would hold her tightly by the hips —she loved that— while silently whispering all the human and inhuman ways I would love her that night. She lived in one of those old warehouses transformed into luxurious lofts, the kind that still bore the original company name at the entrance: Established 1856. Roethlisenberg & Co. We took a spacious freight elevator that opened directly into her apartment, where I fulfilled, to the letter, word for word, everything I had promised her. In the intimacy of her bedroom, which windows were draped with heavy emerald brocade curtains, we could see the tip of the Chrysler Building. The lamps had sensors that turned on with a sigh, the music's volume rose with the intensity of our kisses, and those cool Egyptian cotton sheets captured the scent of our bodies until dawn.

It was the apartment of a real estate agent.

She liked Ella Fitzgerald and Residente, as well as the scented candles she lit by her window. Wine drives me crazy. She always surprises me with playful things wrapping pearl necklaces around her waist, wearing wigs of different colors, transforming into different women. One night, she arrived at Small's in a short dark wig and a long tiger-fur coat. We made love in the bathroom, and yes, I say made love because, at that moment, I felt I loved her with an unfamiliar honesty, even as people pounded on the door. Wine loves to play as much as I do. But soon, she would show me that I was nothing more than a clumsy beginner.

Velha Infância

A heavy storm raged the night Wine came to visit me at my new place in the Village. She arrived around seven, rang the buzzer, and her voice sounded strange like that of a tired woman. She climbed the stairs one by one, as if calculating each step, and I thought maybe she was sick or something. From the doorway, I shouted, "Are you okay?" When I saw her, I realized she was completely soaked. I had bought pizzas and a bottle of Cabernet. She took the bottle and stood there, reading the label, then looked around the apartment in a way that made me wonder if she was high. I went to get a glass of water, some wine glasses, and a corkscrew. Then I took the bottle from her hands and made her drink the water. I sat on the couch, trying to open the bottle between my legs, when Wine unbuttoned her coat and to my surprise, she had nothing on underneath. I thought the Japanese guy might walk into the living room at any moment because I was sure I had heard him in his room. But Wine commanded me to take her right there, on the couch. Still, I kept thinking about the Japanese guy, that with all the noise we were making, he might burst through the door at any second. I grabbed her hand to take her to my room, but she unfastened my pants and slipped her hand inside in such a way that she made me forget every worry in the world. As she did her thing, I thought this could be Spirit, but not Wine. Wine wasn't like this. I closed my eyes while she held me, kissed me, her hands moving over me as she pulled off my shirt, kissed my chest. It was so pleasurable that I completely let go. But then, something felt off. A chill ran down my spine. I opened my eyes, and in one swift motion, I jumped off the couch. The one kissing my chest was the Japanese guy, dressed in a gleaming samurai kimono, glowing in the darkness. With an awkward stance, I prepared to defend Wine, but she stood up and flicked on the lamp. Only then did I see it wasn't the Japanese guy. It was Spirit, dressed as a geisha. "You fool, who do you think got you this cheap room?" she said. Only then did I understand the books, the papers in my room. She had left them for me. Confused, I sat back down because I thought my legs wouldn't hold me for another minute. And with a mischievous spark between us, we continued the game.

I never saw her again after that night.

*

New York is a fantasy, a metropolis of fleeting and forsaken loves seeking conversation in some random bar. I like to remember Wine as a messenger with many faces. She gave me her love, free of fears and complexities, so pure that after her, I felt a newfound strength that helped me keep going in this city. Sometimes, I go back to the liquor store where I first saw her. She was alone, standing by the French wine section, while I searched for a cheap bottle of rum to survive another night in some Midtown shelter. It was at that Wine and Spirit on Lexington and Thirtieth, just a few blocks from the room I now call home, where we first met. I told her I liked the tattoo on her neck, and with her usual gentle smile, she recognized my accent. "Chilean?" she asked. We talked about my trip to Salvador de Bahía, about her trip to Santiago for a theater studies conference. I helped her choose a Carménère, and then we walked downtown, letting the city push us along with its lights, flavors, and shadows. She was a performing arts professor. She had come to New York chasing a hunch, an inexplicable certainty that here, she would find a dream, a hope something that would give her enough strength to return to her city, Natal, after two years of wandering through Europe. "And I found you," she told me, her voice tight, nearly breaking against the cold night air. She was running from something I never knew. I, on the other hand, was simply lost. Near Canal Street, we took the train to Battery Park, then the ferry to Staten Island, where we looked back at Manhattan, no longer an unreachable mirage.

Five days later, she returned to Brazil.

I remember one afternoon, as we watched a ship sail along the East River, she played a song, Velha Infância and we made it ours. We kissed, we laughed, we held each other with the desperate embrace of lovers who already knew the time they would later miss. Sometimes, I have imaginary conversations with Wine, where I tell her about the little things I've managed to achieve in this city, and I think about how beautiful it would have been to spend more time with her. But then I hear that song, our song, and I understand that Wine was a messenger who appeared at just the right moment to give me the strength, the faith I needed to keep going, only to then vanish into the shadows of the skyscrapers of this city I call home.

THE CURIOUS CASE OF THE BICYCLE CANNIBALS

Camila And I

I hadn't noticed the disappearance of the chained-up bicycles on the street until Camila pointed it out. "They're eating them," she shouted from the window overlooking 6th Avenue. "They're eating them little by little." I laughed, imagining delicious bicycles falling victim to some kind of urban cannibalism. I thought it was just another one of her jokes, the kind she makes whenever she's messed something up. "Don't laugh!" she screamed. "They're eating them." And then, she started to cry. Only then did I realize she was serious. I leaned out the window and saw a bike missing a wheel and its seat. I went over to hug her, sat her down on the couch, and opened the window. She needed air. We held each other and sat there in silence. After a few minutes, she walked to the kitchen, grabbed a piece of tissue, dried her tears, and murmured as she disappeared into the bedroom, "They're eating them... little by little."

Since the pandemic began, bicycles have multiplied in Manhattan. The once-wonderful silence of the nights is now interrupted by the whisper of spinning wheels, rattling chains, and electric motors that remind me of urban bumblebees lost in the dark. Most of them belong to delivery workers; a few are used by New Yorkers avoiding public transportation. People lock them up on the streets with chain locks, U-locks, or double chains. But it doesn't matter. The next day, they reappear missing a front wheel, stripped of their seat. Their fate is sealed. Next, the chain disappears. Then the rear wheel, the brake cables, the pedals, the shocks. Day by day, the act of barbarism continues until nothing remains but the frame, still bound to the post like a forgotten corpse. One night, I went out for a walk through the streets of Manhattan, smoking a joint. I saw the skeletal remains of a bike locked up on the sidewalk. It looked like a mutilated body. A wave of nausea hit me, and I had to put out my joint. My skin went clammy as I thought, why don't they take everything at once? Why leave the frame there, rusting away? Is it some kind of warning? The city does nothing. The garbage trucks don't remove them. It's as if they fear something or know something we don't. But our bikes are safe. We keep them in the hallway, right outside our door. Living on the top floor has its advantages. Sometimes I think that if the pandemic had never happened, Camila would never have noticed what was happening to the bicycles.

Before the pandemic, I used to climb up to the rooftop to smoke with Camila. We'd bring a little weed, a bottle of tequila, salt, lime, and go through the ritual; drink, smoke, talk, watch the sky as the smoke faded into the night, swallowed by the towering buildings above us. Our building is only four stories high, and from the rooftop, it feels like sitting in a small valley surrounded by the Andean peaks of New York. So we'd look up, searching for a star we almost never found, or tracing the white scars of airplanes cutting across the darkness. But now that the streets of Manhattan are empty, I drink and smoke down below. The city without people isn't New York. The storefronts remain frozen in time, stuck in March, still advertising winter clearance sales. It's eerie to see mannequins in June dressed in coats and wool hats, men in heavy boots and lumberjack jackets.

Camila wakes up early to tend to her clients in Spain. She's a coach for C-suite executives, and the pandemic has only made her busier. Where she once had two or three sessions a day, now she has three to five. The poor thing never stops. We only come together at night for dinner though even saying "come together" sounds strange, as if we were far apart. She works in our bedroom, the brightest room, with a view of the street. I work in the guest room, which has only a small window facing the building's inner courtyard. Sometimes, I watch my neighbors. Their routines entertain me, and I imagine their lives, like Joe from the third floor, who paces around his kitchen in his underwear, talking on the phone. Then he vanishes, reappears in the living room. Disappears again, then resurfaces in the kitchen to pour himself a cup of coffee. Then he's gone, and the bathroom light flicks on. The girls from the second floor used to walk around naked in the mornings. But ever since the pandemic started, I don't see them anymore. They disappeared, piece by piece, just like the bicycles. First the girls, then Joe, then the others. Now, of the thirty people who used to live in this building, only eight or ten of us remain. I make a living reading birth charts. It started as a hobby, but the pay is so good that I turned it into my job. Acting (my actual profession) has been pushed to the side. I only dedicate a few hours a week to a script I'm writing, a play about a man who lives on the streets, who was once a schoolteacher in Lower Manhattan but, for some reason (which I haven't yet figured out), chooses to leave everything behind and live on the sidewalk. But even that script has been abandoned. These days, I'm too busy, my clients have increased.

Since the pandemic began, Camila and I hardly see each other, despite working in the same apartment. At lunchtime, we heat up a frozen pizza and eat it at our desks. The distance between us has only grown since I laughed when she said the bicycles were being eaten. Our dinners together are almost gone. At night, Camila stays glued to her phone, talking to her family in Florida. Their conversations always circle back to the same things: death counts, the lack of safety measures, and the bicycles that keep disappearing. Then she hangs up and cries into the bed. I've tried to talk to her, but she says she just wants to be alone. So in the afternoons, I go out. I walk, I smoke, I try to clear my head from all this shit. But now, with the quiet, slow devouring of the bicycles, even stepping outside disturbs me.

Bicycles

I don't know what I was thinking when I decided to start taking pictures of the bicycles. On a hard drive, I store every victim I find. I take photos and record videos from different angles to capture their mutilated remains, and file them away in a folder. Day after day, I bear witness to their slow, perhaps even painful disappearance. (What does a bicycle's scream sound like?) Sometimes, I scan the surroundings, searching for clues at the crime scene, something that might explain all of this. At night, I wander through the Village, Soho, Chinatown, Tribeca, even Koreatown with its thick scent of grilled meat, and Battery Park, all the way down in the financial district. Sometimes I return at dawn, at that eerie hour when the few essential workers ride the subway half-asleep, their heads bobbing against the metal poles, giving me the perfect chance to study them. I search their hands, their clothes looking for something, anything, that might give them away. But there's nothing. Sometimes, I imagine Camila listening to me, watching her face soften as I finally tell her who is devouring the bicycles of Manhattan. I've asked friends in Queens, Astoria, Flushing, Sunnyside, Jackson Heights. No mutilated bicycles. Then I asked friends in Brooklyn, Greenpoint, and Williamsburg. Nothing. The bicycles there remain untouched.

Why only in Manhattan?

Now, in the middle of the afternoon, it's beautiful to walk through the wide avenues Madison, Sixth, Park Avenue avenues emptied of cars, of buses, of noise. I've taken advantage of it, stopping by plazas like Union Square, or the smaller ones near playgrounds, to talk to the delivery guys who gather there. I ask them if they've noticed anything about the bicycles. They look tired. And afraid. Deeply afraid. Their eyes dart around with suspicion, their voices muffled behind masks, their words a tangle of half-formed thoughts, sometimes slipping into pure irrationality. When I press for details, they glance at each other, uncertain, then change the subject or simply mount their bikes and disappear in opposite directions. A few, the more methodical ones, give me a thorough breakdown of how they try to protect their bicycles, different kinds of locks, their strengths and weaknesses, small adaptations, adhesive tapes wrapped around the frames. The Mexican riders, in particular, favor tape in the colors of their flag. But in the end, they all agree: none of it matters. "When they want one, they take it." Sometimes, all it takes is leaving the bike locked to a post while running upstairs for a delivery, only to return and find a piece missing, usually the electric battery or the front wheel. And then, like a wounded animal limping through the jungle, the bicycle is tracked, piece by piece, day after day, until all that remains is a skeletal frame, rusting away on the sidewalk.

The saddest ones are the children's bicycles. There's something strange about them. Only the wheels get devoured, the rest is left behind, chained up, rusting under the rain. They can sit there for months, their little bodies abandoned, and no one does anything about it. The delivery guys always have an answer for everything. Sometimes, I get the feeling they know far more than they let on.

"It's bad luck to move those bodies."

"Bad luck?"

"You might get la piña."

"And what's la piña?"

"Do it and you'll see."

Then, once again, they mount their bikes, glance at their phones, and vanish into the eerie silence of Manhattan.

Manhattan is a different place now. You can hear birds singing. I've even seen an eagle perched on a traffic sign, watching, waiting for a rat to scurry through the garbage. Maybe that's why it's easier to notice the mutilated bicycles now. In a normal Manhattan with its tourist chaos, its honking, ambulance sirens, fire trucks, the shouting, and everything else it would be impossible to see them. They've always been there, abandoned, torn apart, their rusted metal exposed to the rain, the snow, the heavy, sticky heat of summer. Two days ago, I called the city to request sanitation services to remove them from the streets. But the operator, in a muffled voice, speaking hurried, almost unintelligible English, said:

"Don't call again."

"Why? Do you know something?"

"Ask the delivery guys" And then he hung up.

The delivery guys? What do they have to do with all of this? It feels like I'm walking in circles. Back at the apartment, Camila stays locked in our bedroom, working all day. She barely goes out, and I can't understand how someone can live like that. I've suggested going for a walk in Central Park. I told her people keep the recommended six-foot distance, that they enjoy the afternoon almost as if everything were normal. But she refuses. She bought a treadmill for nearly eight hundred dollars and uses it every single day. I'd rather run along the Hudson, feel the fresh air coming off the river. Ever since she mentioned the bicycles, things haven't been right. One time, I asked if she was mad about it, and she didn't answer. In bed, it's as if I don't exist. And that worries me. We used to do it two or three times a week. Now, nothing. Not even once. It's stressing me out. Maybe that's why I'm so obsessed with finding out who's eating the bicycles because somehow, in solving this mystery, I might get a part of my life back.

In our apartment, we have two bicycles. We leave them by the door. Mine is a mountain bike, and Camila's is a cruiser with a basket tied to the front, where we usually carry our picnic supplies. We used to go for rides on Saturday mornings and Sunday afternoons, following the Hudson River or sometimes taking the ferry to Staten Island or Brooklyn, exploring neighborhoods that still have that homey feel so different from the tourist-driven Manhattan, where big stores, banks, and chains have swallowed up nearly every small, independent business. Ever since the pandemic began, we haven't gone out. One time, I suggested a ride along the Hudson, all the way to Battery Park, where we could sit and watch the bay. It was a Sunday and she was making lunch. She turned to look at me as if about to say something, but instead, she just stared in silence. And that was when I felt it too. Fear. Her gaze was the same as the delivery guys.' She was cooking pasta. She opened a can of tomato sauce, dumped it into the pot with a sudden, violent motion, and walked to our bedroom, leaving the tomatoes, the garlic, and the carrot untouched on the cutting board.

Two days ago, the camera I ordered online arrived. I set it up by the window, aimed directly at a bicycle being slowly stripped apart. It still had its rear wheel, its chain, and the cables for the gears and brakes. I framed the shot carefully not just to capture the bike but also any details of those taking the parts and left it recording all night. The next morning, I woke up early to check. The bike was the same. On the screen, I saw people walking their dogs, delivery guys passing by, and nothing else.

But today, I finally saw them.

Three figures, draped in white robes, their faces veiled in the same pale color ghostly, weightless, moving like specters through the dimly lit cityscape. They glide toward the bicycles with slow, ritualistic precision, surrounding them in silence. Then, they raise a roughly carved totem that seems to hum with energy as eerie chants echo in the night. One of them pulls tools from a backpack and starts working on the bike's metal frame. But then… The smallest one stops. Turns. And looks straight into the camera. I feel it instantly, his gaze cutting through the distance, slicing through the lens, stabbing into me like a blade of ice. They whisper something to each other, drop their tools onto the ground, and, without hesitation, start walking toward the entrance of my building. Then, the screen goes black. Even though the camera still has battery.

The silence in the apartment becomes unbearable. Slowly, I turn my head toward the door, a cold sweat trickling down my spine.

"Camila!" I call out, my voice barely more than a broken whisper.

"…"

"Camila!" I shout again, louder this time, as I walk toward the apartment door.

With a desperate jolt, I yank it open And there they are. Our bicycles. Shattered. Mutilated. Their remains strewn across the hallway and down the staircase. Camila appears beside me, and the moment she takes in the sight, she collapses to her knees. Her cries send a chill through my skin.

"Oh my God! Oh my God! Our bikes! Those bastards! Our bikes!"she sobs.

I remain frozen, consumed by a twisted mix of fear and rage, gnawing at me, tearing me apart just as our bicycles have been torn to pieces.

Then, suddenly, Camila stands. There is something in her stance, a resolve so sharp, so sudden, that it terrifies me more than anything else. She strides toward the coat rack, grabs her jacket, slips on her shoes, and bolts down the stairs.

"What are you doing?! Camila, what are you doing?! "

She doesn't answer. Not until she reaches the lobby. There, she stops for a moment and looks up at me. For an instant, I think she has come to her senses. But no. She pulls her phone from her pocket and steps outside without a word. Still disoriented, I fumble into my shoes and sprint after her.

Outside, the morning air is thick, heavy, as if the darkness of the night still lingers. I glance one way, then the other. "Camila!" I shout her name toward one street corner, then another. But she's nowhere to be seen. Heart pounding, I lace up my sneakers and run anywhere after her.

ESTEBAN ESCALONA CABA

(Talcahuano, Chile) is an urban writer based in New York City. His first short story collection, Ciudad Capital (2011), was recognized with an award from the Chilean Ministry of Education. In New York, he published Tal Vez Manhattan / Maybe Manhattan (2024), a bilingual collection of chronicles that immerses readers in the overwhelming reality of New York City through the lens of the immigrant experience. His stories and chronicles have appeared in various U.S. literary magazines and anthologies of New York writers, establishing his voice as one of the most distinctive in the city's new urban literature.

www.ingramcontent.com/pod-product-compliance
Lightning Source LLC
LaVergne TN
LVHW090533110826
845146LV00003B/1084

* 9 7 9 8 9 9 9 1 1 4 2 5 9 *